ANTHOLOGY OF CHRISTMAS MEMORIES

EDITED BY DON HART AND
BOB MACKENZIE

Cover illustration and design by Tonya Foreman

ISBN-10: 0615570909
ISBN-13: 978-0-615-57090-7

ACKNOWLEDGMENTS

The authors wish to thank others who provided encouragement and assistance in making this book come to life: Julie Mitchell, Assistant Dean of Special Programs & Continuing Education at the University of Dayton (UD); novelist Nancy Pinard; the officers and staff of the Osher Lifelong Learning Institute at UD; editors Don Hart and Bob Mackenzie; Don Quigley, Mary Ann Hart, Tonya Foreman, Don and Rose Peacock, and Linda Hart for technical help; and the Office of Special Programs & Continuing Education at UD for their kind financial support. We love ya.

FOREWORD

When I agreed to teach creative writing for the University of Dayton's Lifelong Learning Institute (LLI), I pictured ten eager seniors sitting around a large table with enough elbow room and mental space to wander from the kind of left-brain writing they'd done all their academic and professional lives. Alas, it was an old picture—think sepia-toned tin type—borrowed from my first delightful assignment at Sinclair Community College where I was sent off campus to teach at a senior center. Even the LLI coordinator who proposed the class had no idea what would happen. Both of us, too-studied and knowing that learning the craft is hard, imagined few people would sign up for such a class. Together, we wrote a broad-spectrum class description that had me introducing the class to the writing of three genres, fiction, poetry, and memoir, hoping against hope that with all that content, surely, surely, ten seniors would sign up.

The heads-up came when my class list arrived. Sixty-five seniors had signed up to learn three genres in six weeks.

Impossible.

But writers are well-practiced at revision, which literally means *to see again.* I *saw* that it would not be possible to run the class as a single, teacher-guided workshop, the students bringing work to class to read aloud for my instruction and everyone's responses. Equally impossible, time-wise, would be my providing adequate feedback via sixty-five turned-in folders. (Classes of both types have a limit on enrollment.) As an undergraduate, I had always resented classrooms conducted via myriad, unsupervised small groups (the unprepared students leeching off the one who had done the assignment—me—while rendering the trained professional superfluous), but it seemed the only way to handle this class.

The best stories have endings that contain both the element of surprise and a sense of inevitability, including this one. I didn't have a room full of undergraduates. My students were retired professionals, ones who had been schooled in grammar, and who signed up not because this was a required class (or, worse yet, reputed to be an easy A), but *because they were aching to tell their stories.* I stood in front of a packed auditorium, chained to a mike with a cord that threatened to trip me, writing with chalk on an old-time blackboard, able only to skim the surface of three genres, and forced to stand by while they read and edited each other's work. The small groups were so noisy—reading, laughing, enjoying—I could no longer hear the hum of the auditorium's old fluorescent lights. No one had told them writing was hard.

A few of their stories appear in this volume, written at the time or in the months and years that followed. The class formed a writing group at the end of our six weeks together. This is not unusual. Many classes do this. What's surprising is that four years have passed. They are still together, giving each other assignments, writing, and meeting monthly, to read to each other, revise and read again.

I am honored to be called their literary godmother—one who knows the family unwittingly grew too large, who watched in awe while they dressed and bathed one another's work. The word *proud* falls short of what to me is a miracle.

I am humbled to have played a small part.

-Nancy Pinard

Nancy Pinard is the author of two novels, Shadow Dancing (Disc-Us Books, 2000) and Butterfly Soup (Next, 2006). Her short stories have appeared in BELOIT FICTION JOURNAL, THEMA, DOS Passos REVIEW et al., and have been anthologized by The Paper Journey Press and Spinster's Ink.

TABLE OF CONTENTS

PREFACE

Christmas is a time for reflecting and giving. Many of us remember those special times at Christmas that have become conversation pieces for friends and family alike. The short stories, memoirs and poems included in this anthology have been contributed by members of a writers group who have gathered at the University of Dayton each month since 2008.

We hope that you enjoy these works. Maybe they will spark a memory for you as well.

Bob Mackenzie wrote this story for his grandson Anthony, when he was about six years old. When he discovered the truth about Santa, he was very angry! He kept saying that everyone lied to him. This story seemed to help. Many people have read it to their children when they encountered the same situation. In 2009, Anthony died tragically in an automobile accident, at only 19 years old. He still lives his grandfather's heart, and, of course, he always will.

THE GIRL WHO FOUND SANTA
BY BOB MACKENZIE

Once upon a time, not too long ago, there was a girl named Marti who was in love with Santa Claus. Well, she wasn't really in love with him; in fact she never actually met him, not the real Santa.

Like lots of girls and boys, she had visited Santa in various stores. She sat on his lap, had her picture taken with him, and told him what she wanted for Christmas. But all along she knew that those store Santas were not the real Santa. She thought of them as Santa's helpers.

Every year she would get excited about Christmas and wait patiently during Advent for Christmas Eve when Santa would come. She would lie in bed and try to stay awake so she could hear him arrive and maybe get a look at the jolly old guy. But, it never happened. The excitement of the day would get to her and she would fall asleep before he showed up. On Christmas morning she would find presents under the tree and wonder if she would ever meet the real Santa.

It was important to Marti, but not as important as the real meaning of Christmas, which Marti always remembered and celebrated, the birth of Jesus. After all, Jesus had come into the world to free people from their sins and to tell them how much they were loved by His Father. That was an important message that must always be celebrated. Jesus was, after all, a hero greater than any super hero of any age. But still it would be good, Marti thought, to see Santa, just once.

Then it happened, the unthinkable. A friend told Marti that there was no Santa. Marti didn't believe her friend and so she asked her brother Matt.

Matt said, "I guess you're old enough to know. It's true. There is no Santa. Mom and Dad put the presents under the tree each year."

Marti couldn't believe her ears, so she asked her mother in a way that her mother could not deny.

"It's true Marti. Your father and I put the presents under the tree."

Marti was very upset. "How could you lie to me about Santa? How could you let me believe he was real, when you knew he wasn't?"

"Marti," her mother replied, "Santa doesn't exist as a person, but he does exist in our hearts and in our love of giving. We give good gifts to each other in the spirit of Santa. It's not a lie, Marti. It's a tradition based on the great Saint Nicholas. He was a real person who loved to give gifts. Santa, in the tradition of Saint Nick, lives in our hearts. In that way he is alive and real, in our love for each other."

Marti was not happy with this answer. In her mind, it was a lie. Tradition had no meaning to her. "Sounds like just a way to get out of the lie," she thought. Marti was both sad and angry. She had a lot on her mind now. She would have to figure out how to handle this new knowledge. Marti decided on a plan. She would ask her grandma what she thought.

That very day Marti's grandma called her on the phone. "I'm baking cookies today. Would you like to come over and help me?"

Marti loved her grandma and always liked to bake cookies with her.

"Can I go?" Marti asked.

"Yes dear," her mother replied, "I have to go shopping, so I'll drop you off. You go put your coat on."

When Marti arrived, grandma's house was already full of good smells of cinnamon and other spices from several freshly baked pies that were cooling on the counter.

"I'm glad you came over, Marti. We have lots of cookies to bake. Are you ready to get started?"

The way Marti answered her, Grandma knew something was on her mind. "What are you thinking about, Marti?" Grandma asked.

"Oh, I'm kind of upset about Santa. I just found out he's not real, and I'm mad that everybody lied to me about him."

"Lied? What do you mean?" replied Grandma. "Santa is very real, because he lives in our hearts."

"That's what Mom said, but I believed he was a real person, and he's not."

Grandma tried to explain about Saint Nicholas, but Marti told her that her mother had already told her about that and it was not the same. Grandma didn't know what else to say so she got Marti started making cookies and soon Marti forgot about Santa for a while and instead had fun baking.

When her mother came to pick her up, Marti's thinking went back to Santa. Grandma, not knowing what else to do, gave Marti a big hug and a kiss good bye and said, "Try not to let this Santa thing ruin your Christmas. I know it's not the best thing to say, but someday you'll understand, and someday you'll meet the real Santa."

"Oh, Grandma, don't say that," Marti said, sounding somewhat angry.

"No more discussion about it now, dear," Grandma said gently. "Your mother is ready to take you home. Good bye, dear."

Marti left wondering how her grandma could admit that Santa was not a real person and then say Marti would someday meet him. It was all very confusing.

Well, Christmas Eve came and Marti went to bed, but she didn't feel the same. Sure she was anxious to find out what presents she would get from her mother, father, and brother, but she would not try to stay awake for Santa. Growing up was hard. She turned over, feeling sad, and fell asleep.

Christmas morning she woke early, but didn't jump out of bed like she used to. She was somewhat excited, but more like a birthday than Christmas. She put on her robe and slippers and went downstairs to find the tree all lighted and lots of presents to unwrap. There was one large package with her name on it that caught her eye. As she opened it her heart skipped a beat. Just what she wanted. A beautiful large doll stared out of the box at her. It had blond hair that you could curl and a blue velvet dress that was so soft to the touch. It was the one thing that Marti really wanted and was afraid she would not get because it was so expensive, and since there was no Santa her parents would have to pay for it.

Marti knew about money and how you sometimes had to save a long time to get the things you wanted. Her grandpa had told her about that.

"I will keep you forever," she said to the doll. "I don't care what else I get, as long as I have you. I will name you Mary. That's a beautiful name."

And so Marti was both happy and sad at the same time. She got what she wanted, but not from Santa. Marti's mother, father, and brother came downstairs and Marti told them how happy she was for the doll. It felt strange to thank her parents for the presents. Before, there was no need to thank Santa.

After all the presents were opened and breakfast was eaten, Marti and her family got ready to go to Mass to celebrate the real meaning of Christmas.

"Can I take my doll?" Marti asked.

"Yes, dear," her mother said. "When we get there you can let her sit in the pew with you, but you must pay attention to the services."

That seemed fair to Marti, for Marti had a very keen sense of fair play. And so they all got into the car and started for church. Just as they drove onto the freeway, they saw flashing red and blue lights ahead. Traffic was almost stopped. Marti's father, who was a volunteer fireman, pulled the car over to the side of the road and got out to see if he could help. In the excitement, no one noticed that Marti also got out and followed her father up the side of the road, firmly holding her doll.

"Hi Jim," a man in uniform said to Marti's father. "It's a bad one. There's a little girl trapped in the car and she's bleeding pretty badly. We're doing what we can, but we can't calm her down. The bleeding would slow if we could get her calm."

"What can I do?" Marti's father asked.

"Not much, Jim, we've got all the equipment here, but I feel so bad for the little girl. If only she would calm down."

"Can I talk to her, Daddy?"

Marti's father was startled to hear her voice. "Marti, why aren't you in the car?"

"Daddy, don't be mad. Let me talk to her. Maybe I can calm her down."

"It might help, Jim," said the man in uniform.

And so they took Marti to the car. She could see the little girl through the broken window. At first Marti was almost sick from the sight. The little girl's face was covered with blood.

"Oh, Daddy," she said, "she's really hurt bad."

"Maybe you should go back to our car," her father said."

"Let me try to talk to her first," Marti pleaded.

Marti tried to talk to the little girl, but the girl would not calm down. Then Marti tried singing, which always worked with her baby cousins.

"Twinkle, twinkle, little star," she sang, but the little girl would not calm down. She would only stretch out her arms and scream. Then Marti realized that the little girl was reaching for her doll.

"Oh no," thought Marti, "not my new doll. No, I can't give you my new doll. I promised to keep her forever."

Marti was sad in her heart for the little girl. Her mind whirled, "The little girl would do better if she were calm, but my new doll?"

As Marti watched the little girl reach and reach, her heart melted. With a tear in her eye she unlocked her arms from around the doll, took it in her hands, and reached it into the little girl.

The little girl stopped screaming and began to sob quietly.

Marti looked at her and smiled through her own tears, "Her name is Mary." She said. "She's brand new."

The girl became calmer. As she hugged the doll, the blood from her face rubbed off on the doll's beautiful golden hair, staining it red. Soon the girl was free of the wreck, and the man in uniform came over to talk to Marti and her father.

He looked at Marti, "You were a big help, honey. And you even gave your Christmas doll away. You're a regular Santa."

"What," thought Marti, "I'm a Santa? Me a Santa?"

At once she remembered her grandma's words, "Someday you'll meet the real Santa."

At last Marti understood that Santa lives in her heart and that when she gave out of love and compassion for others, she became the real Santa.

This story is one of 20 chapters in an unpublished memoir by Don Hart, entitled How Not to Run Away from Home. *Each chapter is a stand-alone short story. This story describes a small boy's bewilderment when he discovers that what he always believed about "magic" is just not true.*

THE MAGIC SET
BY DON HART

Long ago, about a month before Christmas, I personally witnessed a miracle. It was performed by my Uncle Melvin when he was 22 years old, and I was only seven. It was truly a fantastic, incomprehensible and awe-inspiring act.

Uncle Melvin took my hat and effortlessly made it "disappear" right before my eyes!

To a young boy well schooled in Christian training, who fervently believes in miracles, getting to see one up close was just astonishing.

"Was that a miracle?" I asked.

"No," he laughed, "it was just magic. Do you want to search me to see if I have it on me somewhere?"

"Yeah, I guess so." I checked everywhere he suggested.

"How did you do that?

"I tucked my head down and grumbled a few magic words, and 'poof!' It just vanished."

"Can you tell me those words?

"No, you don't understand. Magicians never tell their secrets. If they did, it would ruin their magic."

"But I won't tell anyone else the magic words," I promised.

"Can't do it," he said, and then with a few words and a wide motion, he made my hat reappear!

I was dumbfounded at this wondrous thing! I pressed him more for the magic words he used to make this happen.

"Are the words you used to make it come back the same as the ones you used to make it go away?"

"No, they were different," he said.

"Could you teach me some magic?"

"Ask your Dad. He's been known to pull a few rabbits out the hat now and then."

***

I was so impressed with my uncle's 'miracle,' err, magic, that I could not get it out of my mind. I talked with a few of my friends about magic, and my friend Bill told me he went to a magic show once and actually saw a magician pull a live rabbit out of his hat. Maybe magic had something to do with hats? I pressed Bill for more information about the magician he saw:

"What words did he say?"

"I don't know," said Bill. "If your uncle said your Dad could do that too, why don't you ask him?"

This whole business of magic was becoming my new obsession. Bill told me he had been to a toy store the weekend before and saw a Magic Set in a box.

"Wow! What's in the box?"

"Just magic stuff, like a wand and some metal rings, I don't know. I didn't look inside. This Christmas I just want a Schwinn. They're the best bikes made."

***

When I got my Dad alone, I told him what Uncle Melvin did and asked him if he could "pull a rabbit out of a hat."

"Well I did a few times for your uncle, but I hope I won't have to do it for you very often, at least not until you get older."

There it was again, that put-off all kids get all the time. I always got it from older people. That "wait till you get older" stuff. And, in those days it took years and years of waiting to "get older." Nowadays, I can do it in fifteen minutes.

That year, after I told my Dad I wanted a Magic Set for Christmas, it took something like twenty years before the middle November turned into late December. He told me if I were good there was a chance Santa Claus would bring me one.

"Could you just get me the Magic Set, Daddy? I don't know about Santa anymore."

"Haven't you been good this year?" he asked.

"Yeah, I think so, but some of the older kids are telling me there is no Santa Claus."

"You tell them they are *wrong*! And if you want magic in your future, there's the guy who really has it."

"Really?"

***

When Christmas finally came, my Dad told me there was something left under the tree for me from Santa. Sure enough, a big box said **Magic Set** on the outside. It had five small red balls inside and a red cup the exact size of half of a ball, a wand, a half dozen stainless steel rings, some colorful silk handkerchiefs and a Magic Instruction Book.

The first thing I did was pounce on that book! The book had pictures of how to do tricks by fooling people. And these instructions were very hard to read. *Where were the magic words?*

No magic words.

Didn't powerful wizards and witches and fairy godmothers and hypnotists say magic words and then marvels happened? Didn't Santa Claus himself use magic words to get his big body down a chimney? Didn't witch doctors and fortune tellers and charmers I saw at the fair use magic words all the time? Didn't my priest at church say words that changed bread into the presence of God? Didn't powerful people use words that caused great changes to happen? And what about Uncle Melvin?

I told my Mom, but she did not seem to understand me. When I told my Dad he understood perfectly that this was indeed a crisis situation. He told me that words do sometimes have magic and could cause huge changes, but I was too young then to fully understand the power of faith, and the incredible joy and hurt spoken words can cause.

He noticed I had shown no more interest in my Magic Set.

"Why don't you try to learn some of the tricks?" he asked me.

"They are just too hard for me to do. I thought they would be easy with magic words."

One of the steel rings had a thin cut which allowed it to hook up to the other rings, but the cut was so closely gauged, an audience could not tell how the magician joined the rings. I told him I could do this trick, but not well.

"Then practice a long time and use the magic word that will always work if you need something to change like magic."

"What's that word?" I asked him.

"The word is 'Donald.'"

'Donald' is my real name. He said the word and then performed the ring trick faultlessly. It took me a while to catch on. I learned I had to practice a lot to make any act look enchanting. And, I had to depend on myself to make the magic in my life.

"Actions are much more important than magic words...most of the time," he told me.

CHRISTMAS SCREWED
BY MARTHA WILLIS

It was a very exciting day. We were driving to downtown Louisville in my Daddy's new 1942 Hudson to Sears Roebuck's parking lot to pick out a Christmas tree. We did this every year and even though I was only seven, I recalled times we had done it before – it seemed *forever ago.*

My 12-year-old sister, Nancy, and I could barely contain ourselves.

Our favorite time of year, Christmas carols playing on the radio, picking out the tree and, of course, we would buy candy at the Sears candy counter. I loved the gummy orange slices, and Nancy always picked the icky circus peanuts.

Our beautiful tree rode on the top of the car, tied on with clothes line. At home Daddy took the tree downstairs to put it on a stand and rearrange the branches. He always liked to cut some branches off and put them in another place on the tree trunk by drilling holes and gluing them in. I think, because he was a dentist, he liked to do things like that.

Daddy proudly brought it to the living room, trailing sawdust footprints on the maroon rug. He told us to get the ornaments while he put on the colored lights.

We returned to the living room and under Mother's watchful eye, we unwrapped the precious ornaments. My favorites were the little fat Santas in red, fur-trimmed suits playing horns and drums.

I also loved the little horn with a red velvety ribbon that really made a sound when you blew into it. There were beautiful shiny, round balls colored red and green, silver and gold that reflected the lights at night.

Mother put the crafts we had made at school front and center. Each homemade ornament was admired and memories revisited.

We ended our task of decorating with long strands of silver tinfoil draped carefully over each branch. Mother stopped us from throwing wads of ice cycles from tired, small hands. She wanted it to be perfect.

At last, it was complete. The tree stood by the big window that looked out onto the front porch. Mother decided it needed to be moved so it would be right in the middle of the window. She tugged gently on the large branches several times and it didn't budge. She told Nancy to go call Daddy so he could help move it over.

When Daddy entered the room, we all beamed proudly and he admired the decorated tree. It glowed with colorful lights, shimmering ice cycles, and all the traditional and much loved ornaments.

Mother asked him to move the tree closer to the center of the window. And he proudly said, "We can't move the tree! I screwed the tree to the floor and this year it won't move or tip over as it often has in the past. Isn't that great!"

Mother's face was memorable.

Nancy and I tiptoed back to our room and closed the door. I'll never forget the Christmas of 1942. And I've often wondered if that house still has the holes in the hardwood floor from that long ago Christmas season.

A version of this story was published in Kitchen Table Stories: A Story Circle Network Anthology of Stories and Recipes (The Story Circle Network, 2007).

CHRISTMAS DAY SAUSAGE BREAD
BY JUDY WHELLEY

Our annual Christmas Day Open House began the year my husband and I created our own Christmas celebration for our son. Prior to this, we usually travelled from Ohio to Pennsylvania to one of the grandparents' houses for the big day. We decided to postpone the out-of-town family travel until December twenty-sixth so our son could open his gifts at home. With no immediate family in the area yet still craving the joy of a full house on Christmas, we extended an invitation to all our local friends – just come, anytime! And so a new tradition began.

I wanted to serve food that was appropriate no matter the time of day, was served hot, and was easy to prepare yet delicious. I remembered a sausage bread that I enjoyed at a friend's house some years before. The recipe was found and duly prepared. That sausage bread was devoured by all with rave reviews. As the years went by, it became an integral part of the celebration. I baked about a dozen loaves throughout the day. The first guests usually arrived around noon and the last left around ten. Friends planned their visits to overlap with one another. It became a day rich with love, laughter, and sharing.

When my husband and I separated, the first question after the initial shock was, "What about your Christmas Open House and the *sausage bread*?" I assured all that the tradition would continue. The first year was hard. It is difficult to see a long marriage end, and friendships needed to be adjusted. Over the years some friends fell by the wayside and others came to take their place. But sausage bread and affection ruled the day. The tradition was strengthened and continues.

19

Christmas Day is the only time I bake this bread. I share the recipe freely, but my friends claim it never tastes as good as it does when they have it at my home. I tell them the secret ingredient is the love I have for them mixed with the magic of Christmas Day.

Christmas Day Sausage Bread

Ingredients:
 ½ pound grated Cheddar or Colby cheese
 1 teaspoon garlic salt
 1 teaspoon dried parsley
 3 eggs (save ½ of one to brush on top)
 ¼ pound grated Swiss cheese
 2 tablespoons grated Parmesan cheese
 2 packages crescent rolls
 1 pound bulk sausage (regular, hot, or combination
  according to taste)

Preparation:
 Preheat the oven to 350 degrees F
 Combine the first six ingredients.

Pinch the crescent rolls together to make 2 large (or 4 small) rectangles. Sprinkle (or mash) sausage over each rectangle. Then spread the egg cheese mixture over each and pat down. Roll each rectangle like a jellyroll, starting at one of the long edges. Place each roll, seam side down, in a glass baking dish. Tuck under the ends and brush tops with the reserved egg.

Bake 35-45 minutes. Allow to cool slightly before serving.

Makes 2 large or 4 small loaves. Loaves can be frozen after cooling. Thaw before reheating.

*How do you **really** feel about Christmas? Some people will surprise you. While most agree there is plenty of seasonal joy, social statistics reveal a "down side" or even "dark side" also. Rose Peacock, who is married to Don Peacock, another of our authors in this anthology, gives a wider look at Christmases past. Here she presents one chapter of her Memoir, describing a few candid memories – not all jolly.*

CHRISTMAS
BY ROSE PEACOCK

Christmas. What a dreadful, wonderful, depressing, magical holiday. Christmas is the most interfering, intoxicating, bank-breaking time of the year, sometimes providing total elation or total depression. Most people decorate, celebrate, exchange gifts, attend parties, and hopefully never forget that this is the day when the most unique individual ever known to mankind was born.

I don't think I like Christmas. I love buying trees, ornaments and decorations. I hate putting them on the tree along with all the other areas to be decorated. I love giving presents. I hate receiving them. They are always the wrong size, wrong color or something I would never buy for myself or want.

I love going to Christmas parties. I hate giving them. I love eating the elaborate dinners. I hate preparing them and cleaning up after them. I love receiving Christmas cards and hearing from friends and family. I don't hate, but I don't like, addressing Christmas cards and writing notes. My hand always cramps and my writing becomes unreadable. I don't particularly like receiving one-size-fits-all Christmas letters. No sane person or family is that happy, healthy or successful. I always want to write them back and tell them Johnny finally passed his remedial reading test.

I love the beautiful snow. I hate shoveling the snow and even more the accidents it causes. And I really don't like snow when it gets dirty and black. Who needs a "white Christmas"?

I love getting together with family and friends. I hate the pain caused by the illnesses and death of loved ones or friends.

All churches look beautiful at Christmas and some of them put on wonderful pageants. I try to go to as many as possible: Christian Life Center, the Baptist church in Springfield, St. Mary's Catholic church to see their manger scene. One year I was in California on business and went to the Crystal Cathedral with a very devout associate. We sat in the balcony so we could see everything. He was enthralled with the story. I was wondering where in the hell was that angel going to land. And I hoped the camel wouldn't spit. My time as docent for the Cincinnati Zoo had taught me camels do not like to walk near walls. My concern was unfounded – the camel was a good camel and did not spit.

Decorating is another wonderful thing at Christmas and the decorations vary in different parts of the country. So much more decorating outside can be done in warm climates. But no matter what part of the country is being decorated, the decorating should have a plan. Most folks do not have a plan – just the decorations. And they use all of them.

Over my lifetime I have had all kinds of Christmas trees with all kinds of decorations. Real live trees, artificial trees, aluminum trees, feather trees and/or flocked trees decorated in various ways. All blue lights and ornaments, all red, all green, all mixed up. But always carefully decorated with each item placed just so. Usually Don and I have at least two trees, sometimes more. One traditional, one with all handmade ornaments, one with all sheep ornaments, and one with all nautical ornaments.

One of the memorable Christmases we had was the time our Siamese cat knocked the tree over three times. The house had an entryway with a staircase going up from it. The staircase had a wide banister that the cat could sit on. She did so except in the middle of the night she leaped from the banister into the tree and of course the tree fell over. She thought this was fun and did it three nights in a row. We gave up and took the tree down.

Yes, most of the ornaments were broken. Yea – we can buy more!

Another was the tree one of our cats liked to climb – we took a picture of the cat in the tree and used it for our Christmas card.

All of the cats like to sleep under the tree and we always put ornaments near the bottom of the tree that they can knock off and play with. However they really don't want those – they want the ones that are expensive and break.

Then there was the Christmas my older sister Dorothy and I were home by ourselves. Mom and her sister had gone to California to visit their sister and my brother. On the way home I wrecked the car and was really upset. Dorothy said not to worry - she had bought a holly man decoration on her way home and he would look really cute under the tree. We passed that holly man back and forth for years.

After Don and I were married and moved north we frequently had carolers come by horse drawn wagon. And frequently we went to Louisiana for Christmas. The trip down was usually uneventful but coming back was another story. One return trip was marked by Don driving on ice from northern Alabama to north of Nashville. We watched semis go off the road on both sides of the interstate. We drove on the median, on the berm and didn't stop for anything. Just kept going. Only took about 17 hours to drive home from Nashville.

Now that we are old there is the annual discussion – should we exchange presents or not? After all we have everything we need or want. Should we decorate or not? If so, how much? One tree or all of them? Outside or just inside? What if it is cold and snowy or rainy? What if all the neighbors decorate and we don't? Who cares! What did you get me?

This story is a chapter in Harry Leahy's as yet unpublished memoir about his experiences in 1944 as a postulant in the Society of Mary. In this piece, Harry is only 15 years old, attending high school at Mount Saint John. It centers on a Midnight Mass and other boyish interests during the final months of World War II.

CHRISTMAS 1944
BY HARRY LEAHY

JOY TO THE WORLD is belted out by Brother Charles, a tenor, THE LORD HAS COME. As the lights come on, the night time noises, sneezes, sniffles, coughs and farts are quieted, while the banging of the steam pipes continues. LET EARTH RECEIVE HER KING! I roll over and stick my feet out from under the warm blanket into the cold air of the dormitory at Mount St. John. LET EVERY HEART PREPARE HIM ROOM.

This will be my third Christmas away from home, or rather at my new home as a fifteen-year-old high school student, a postulant, studying to be a teaching brother. I had "left The World."

We had gone to bed a little earlier than the usual time, 9:30 PM, since it was Christmas Eve. I knew we'd wake with song, rather than the clanging of the bell by the prefect from previous years, but still, it was a thrill. AND HEAVEN AND NATURE SING, HEAVEN AND NATURE SING!

The cold of the dorm came as a bit of shock, and a quick face wash and trip to the toilet got me moving. Outside there was about ten inches of snow, in which we hoped to have fun during the studies break between the two holidays. We had already made the toboggan path from the top of the hill to the main gate. The next thing was to head to chapel for Christmas Midnight Mass, where the young brothers and scholastics were already singing carols. AND HEAVEN AND NATURE SING!

There was a Solemn High Mass with three priests, incense and Gregorian chant. PUER NATUS EST NOBIS ET FILIUS DATUS EST NOBIS. I didn't understand Latin, but I really enjoyed chant and could read the words pretty quickly, even without any understanding. As Mass progressed something changed outside, and I became aware of something unusual.

The quiet of the snow-covered landscape was broken with the claps of thunder and flashes of lightning followed by a downpour, unexpected in December. The storm continued, somewhat diminishing as Mass went on, but it really was a distraction, ruining all hopes for fun in the snow. PEACE ON EARTH, GOOD WILL TO MEN.

After Mass we got to open any presents sent by our parents, sharing cookies and candies from our "mush boxes." Finally it was time to head back to bed for the rest of the night.

Morning came and Christmas day started, all slowly rising again in the cold dormitory. The sun was shining and the wind had turned to north, while the outside temperature fell to near single digits. The wet snow, mostly soaked through to the ground, turned to ice. Not much was moving anywhere in the area.

Well, that turned our hope of tobogganing to ice-skating, which became our sport and exercise for the rest of the week. Initially we were able to skate not only on the property, but also on the country roads without thought of traffic. Some of us skated half way to Xenia.

Under supervision of Brother George, our Prefect, we developed an ice rink on the shaded north side of the main building. That rink lasted most of January, even into February with flooding on cold nights, allowing lots of skating time during recreation periods. To say so myself, I got pretty good at skating.

While I was delighting in this fantasy surrounding the annual celebration of the birth of a baby Jew, Jesus, "The

World" about me that Christmas of 1944 was devolving into death and destruction. World War II was in progress and the Battle of the Bulge raged on elsewhere, where freezing cold and rain were experienced much differently.

My cousin Joe was facing V-1 and V-2 rockets in England, while his brother Ray was hiding in foxholes on islands in the Pacific.

In another land, the German Army was inducting Hitler Youth, young boys my age, some even as young as twelve, willing and unwilling, into their armed forces for their last ditch stand. One of these was a seventeen-year-old by the name of Joseph Aloysius Ratzinger, later Pope Benedict XVI.

Meanwhile the fullest extent of the genocide of the Jewish people, The Holocaust, and execution of thousands of others continued, only later to become common knowledge.

Four months – thirty years – after *that first Christmas*, again a celebration of sorts proceeds yearly, with its own music and drama, DEUS, DEUS MEUS, RESPICE IN ME: QUARE ME DERELIQUISTI? That same celebrated person, the baby, now a Man, the Prince of Peace, is dying on a cross.

One of his last words was, "Father forgive them, they don't know what they do."

Will we, or more importantly, *can we*, ever learn?

Brother Charles later became Father Charles Lees, SM. He did at least one of the three years I spent at Mount St. John, but his voice remains in my mind all these years.

Brother George refers to Br. George Dury, SM. He was Prefect of Postulants for many a year, the three years I spent there included. What he missed in height he made up for in zest for whatever he was involved in.

Neona Eloy was the Facilitator for Fostercare and Adoptions at St. Joseph Children's Treatment Center for over 25 years until its closing. She served a special needs population of children suffering from emotional disturbances, usually brought on by abuse and/or neglect. The Gift is from a collection of her poems centered on that experience. These works are her attempt to understand, and communicate to others, the plight of many children in our community.

THE GIFT
BY NEONA ELOY

"What would you like for Christmas?"
    He asked,
"Perhaps a little boy?"
He's somewhat of a handful,
but he'll bring you so much joy
He sleeps all night, especially,
if he's fed right, and on time
He eats at 8, 10, 2 and 4,
and finishes up at 9.

"What would you like for Christmas?"
    He asked,
To make your day complete?
A perfect little man, perhaps,
would sweep you off your feet.
Of course he's just a wee bit slow
and won't stand still a minute
And you'll have to hide your purse,
you know,
Or look for nothing in it.

"What would you like for Christmas?"
    He asked,
"The time is drawing near"
When life takes on a magic glow,
and all are of good cheer
When children like our Sammy, here,
though cruel, at times, need love
Especially from a Mommy Dear,

whose heart he cannot move.

"What would you like for Christmas?"
        He asked,
"Another shiny toy?"
Some electronic thing to break your heart
when you could mend a boy?
Would you rather have your dreams
wrapped up in silver foil or gold?
Or, draped in flesh so fragile—
that only Love can hold.

This story was written as therapy by Don Hart around Christmas 2010 when he felt "terribly wronged" by a local bank. Here's hoping you will enjoy his madcap revenge fantasy crafted by an experienced elf.

THE SUBORDINATE CLAUS
BY DON HART

It was the day before Christmas Eve. Charlie was returning home from Fussmann Sweeper Company's annual Christmas party, where he had played Santa Claus for the eleventh year in a row. As he drove past the Feathered National Bank, his mood darkened. These were the guys who manipulated him into "extra charges" and stole critical pin money he needed for a good Christmas. On pure impulse, he decided to rob the place.

The robbery was not well planned. He just drove into the branch parking lot in his own car, dressed in his Santa suit, put on his whiskers, walked into the lobby with his red cloth bag, and demanded money from the teller. Her name was Karen. She looked quite alarmed, at least when he first went to her station with his Christmas get up.

"You owe me $113," he told her.

She laughed out loud, which seemed to relax the other tellers and the manager across the room. The manager had started to reach under her desk for the red button that notifies the police. When the teller acted amused, and laughed, the manager withdrew her hand, and began looking at a bank report. People often come into banks dressed up around Christmas and Halloween.

"Just put it in this bag," Charlie said quietly.

His hand was under the bag on the counter and Karen thought she saw a glint of metal, which might have been a gun.

33

"I always do whatever Santa tells me."

The teller started pulling bundles of 10's and 20's from her drawer. She asked him to give her the bag so she could fill it with money.

Charlie said, "No, I want you to count out $113 exactly, nothing bigger than a twenty."

"Here's a $1000 she said nervously."

"No, dammit, I said $113 exactly, and you can keep the dye pack."

Finally, Karen counted out the amount he asked for. He checked it and it was a dollar over. He handed the extra dollar back to her. Then he walked out and got into his car. That was when she reached under the counter and pushed her red button. The cameras had been running the whole time.

Charlie drove a few blocks south and looked for a good place to park his car. He could already hear police sirens. He found a spot in an alley behind an old storage barn, where he took off his Santa suit and whiskers and threw them in the back seat. Then he took the $113 out of the red bag and looked around the area. He threw the empty bag inside the car. No one saw him as best as he could tell.

He walked about a mile back home and called the police.

"This is Charlie Uhl calling. Somebody took my car. I don't know when they took it. I had a few personal things in there too."

After he gave the police a full description of the car and his plate number, he thought he heard some commotion on the other end of the phone line.

"Sir, can we get your address?"

"Sure," said Charlie.

After he gave them his address, the policeman asked him, "What were the *few personal things* you left in the car?"

"Well, a Santa Claus suit, a bag of groceries and a twelve pack of beer."

"Stay put, sir, we'll send a crew right out."

A new police cruiser with two bright looking officers was at his door within ten minutes.

"Wow, your guys got here quick," Charlie said as he welcomed them through his front door.

He noticed one of the officers kept his hand on his gun, which he found unusual. He also noticed this officer kept looking over every inch of his living room while the older officer talked.

"Now where did you leave your car?"

"Right out front… in the driveway."

"About what time did you notice it missing?"

"About a half hour ago."

"Where were you in your car before you parked it?"

"I was on a job," Charlie said. He may have chosen his words carelessly. The officer perked up immediately on hearing this.

"What kind of job?"

"Well, it was a company party at Fussmann Sweeper. I was playing Santa Claus for all the kids."

"So you wore the Santa suit for the job at Fussmans?"

"Be kinda hard to play Santa Claus without it," said Charlie with a twinkle.

"OK, OK, when did you take off the suit?"

"I took it off after I made my exit from all the kids."

"And when exactly was that?"

"After they all got their presents."

"No, No. What time was that? And where?"

"About 3:00 o'clock maybe. In Mr. Fussman's office."

"You didn't drive away with the suit on?"

"Heck no," said Charlie. "Those kids thought I was flying out with reindeer power from Fussman's factory roof. I sure wouldn't want any of them see Santa drive away in a banged up Ford."

"What made them think you were leaving there from the roof?"

"My elf probably told 'em! Kids always want to know where Santa's reindeer are, how he got there and how he's leaving for the North Pole. I always find someone at these parties to dress up in a green outfit and help out as an elf. You remember how the joke goes: your elf becomes a "subordinate Claus."

Charlie noticed the older officer blushing, not expecting a joke. He saw several stripes on his sleeve and assumed he was a sergeant. The other officer stayed a distance watching carefully, one hand on his hip, the other on his gun, looking ready to shoot on command.

"You keep a gun in this house, Mr. Uhl?"

"Yeah, I got one in the closet. But, I wasn't planning on using it on the jerk that stole my car."

"Show us where."

Charlie took them to his bedroom closet and pulled out an old shotgun. The sergeant checked to see if it was loaded while the younger officer eyeballed every bit of his bedroom.

"Where's the ammo for this?

"Shot it all up about two years ago, last time I went hunting."

"Any other guns?

"Nope."

They went back and sat down again in Charlie's living room.

"Now that car of yours," asked the sergeant, "when did you last see it?"

"When I got out of it."

"Why did you leave your suit and your keys and a bunch of groceries in the car when you got out of it?"

"I only had a small bag of groceries and some beer. The keys are right he..." Charlie looked on the table near the door.

"Oh, I usually take the keys out of the car and put 'em here. I guess I didn't do that today."

"Why not?"

"Well, when I got out of the car after getting back home, I was in a powerful hurry to get into the house."

"You were? And why was that?" asked the sergeant.

"Had a *mighty urge* from nature. Happens some times when you get old like me."

"How'd you get in the house?"

"Walked through the front door, actually *ran through* it."

"Don't you lock it?'

"Most of the time, no, there's nothing worth stealing in here. But, I didn't mean to leave my keys in the car."

Both the officers turned their heads toward each other and nodded slightly.

"Mr. Uhl, do you have picture of your car?"

"Nawh, it ain't the kind of car that oughta be in pictures. It's really sort of ugly, but all I can afford. You think you'll be able to find it for me?

"We'll see." As the sergeant stood up, the young officer stood also. His hand was no longer on his gun.

"Well, thanks," said Charlie, as he showed them out. "Merry Christmas."

After they left, Charlie wrote out notes on their discussion. He knew he'd be asked the same questions again, so he wanted to be sure the next time he talked with police, his answers would be the same.

***

The state patrol found Charlie's car late on Christmas Eve. It was thirty miles from where Charlie abandoned it. They told Charlie the car was used in a bank robbery and the FBI had impounded it as evidence. It might be sometime before he could get it back.

He later found out there were no groceries inside, but there was a Santa suit and a set of whiskers. The car was also full of empty beer bottles and multiple sets of fingerprints. Maybe some local teenagers had given it a *test drive.*

On Christmas Day at about 10:45 AM Charlie was in church and was praying that God would protect him from the FBI. It was either a coincidence or synchronicity, if you have studied Carl Gustav Jung, that two different computer servers, in two different locations of the Feathered National Bank fritzed out at that exact moment. Thousands of personal check account statements from early in the year were obliterated, along with a few hundred letters connected to those accounts. *Probably an Act of God.*

One of those letters, addressed to a Mr. Charles Uhl, for example, read as follows:

IMPORTANT   NOTICE   ABOUT   YOUR ACCOUNT OVERDRAFT

PLEASE BE AWARE THAT YOUR ACCOUNT WAS OVERDRAWN ON FEBRUARY 15 IN THE   AMOUNT   OF $1.19.   NO   ITEMS CONTRIBUTING TO THE OVERDRAFT WERE RETURNED, AND YOUR ACCOUNT WAS CHARGED $33.00 IN OVERDRAFT FEES TODAY. TO AVOID BEING CHARGED AN $8.00 FEE FOR EACH DAY YOU WERE OVERDRAWN, YOU WILL NEED TO MAKE A DEPOSIT AS SOON AS POSSIBLE.

WE   URGE   YOU   TO   TAKE   ACTION IMMEDIATELY TO AVOID FUTURE OVER-DRAFTS,   RETURNED   ITEMS,   PENALITIES AND FEES.

A little background information is useful here. By the time Charlie got the bank's letter in the mail, about ten days later, it was already February 25th. But everything worked out fine, at least for the bank. Charlie's immediate deposit squared up his account, by leaving him $113 short! He guessed this was the interest the bank collected over 10 days on a dollar and nineteen cents. This was about a gazillion percent more than the Carlo Gambino Juice Company ever collected from their customers. That was the day when Charlie's anger began to burn.

After a protracted argument with the bank manager, Charlie closed his account. She would not budge. *Bank regulations*, you know. For the next 10 months, anytime Charlie heard the bank's commercials or drove by one of their branches, he cursed that bank again. On December 23rd he pounced, not really sure why it happened then. He hoped the manager did not remember him when he had to rob her bank just to reclaim his money.

Luckily, nobody at the bank seemed to recognize Charlie when his picture was shown around later. He *had* been wearing a disguise during the "hold-up." The teller was the only one who thought he could "maybe" be the bank robber. No one volunteered any help, and one of the outside camera lenses was dirty. The bank's security team was discouraged by management from getting involved this particular robbery.

The FBI was a different story. They interviewed Charlie three times and took his fingerprints. They investigated his background deeply and found him to be solvent, sober and a good citizen.

But, the amount bothered them. Why would anyone want to steal a car to rob a bank for $113? OK, so a man about the size of Charlie Uhl, who could wear his Santa suit, robs a bank, but why did he have to look so much like Charlie on the security films? They were dealing with a well-regarded man almost 80 years old, who had no criminal record. His story was always the same as he first told it to the local police. He never wavered or acted guilty. Things checked out when he told them he had no account with this bank.

The U.S. Attorney also had problems...with the time

frames. How could Mr. Uhl abandon his own car 30 miles from the robbery and get back home in time to call the police? None of the prints on the beer bottles led to teenage joy riders. He sent the agents out to recheck Charlie's movements on the day of the robbery. Fussman Sweeper Company executives laughed in their faces when they said the FBI seriously doubted Charlie's alibi.

The bank was strangely uncooperative. The teller named Karen was flighty and changed her story twice; the prosecuting attorneys thought she would make a terrible witness. There was nothing but circumstantial evidence. No weapon. No useful witnesses. The case was closed by the following April, right about the time of Charlie's birthday. But no one at the FBI bothered to tell him.

He went to the post office on April 7th to pick up a birthday package from his daughter who lived in Canada. She was such a thoughtful girl. She had been asking him for over a year to come and live with her. It sure is nice to feel *wanted*, thought Charlie.

While waiting in line, he glanced over the gallery of criminals posted on the wall for the FBI. That was the day Charlie decided to leave town and go live with his daughter. He also decided right then to retire permanently from the Santa Claus business.

Charlie was looking at a grainy picture on the wall of a bank robber in a Santa Claus outfit standing in the lobby of a bank. He knew the face quite well. Under his picture it said, **MOST WANTED.**

Christmas can be a difficult time for teachers, especially the dedicated ones. Holidays mean special activities and traditional events. A good teacher acquaints students with what is important in our culture. Sometimes, that teacher's personal life gets shuttled aside in the effort to do well.

A TEACHER'S CHRISTMAS ANGEL
BY VIRGINIA EVERS

The huge Christmas Surprise Box was dragged out from the coatroom and lifted high up on the table in the front of the classroom. Eager seven-year olds wondered about the mysteries that could be found inside.

With a glint in her eye, Mrs. Lee smiled at her class. "Thanksgiving is over. The turkeys, pilgrims, and Indians have been put away for this year. Now is the time to prepare for the birthday of Jesus," she said.

Out of the box came enough white lunch bags for each child. They were to put their names on them, and books, stickers, and prizes would be put inside. After they were decorated, they would line the windowsill until Christmas vacation.

Next came two calendars. One was an Advent calendar. Each day a child would open the number of the date and a symbol of Advent would appear. The other calendar was numbered 1-24. Each day a child would move the mouse one step closer to Jesus' birthday on December 25.

Mrs. Lee was getting very tired thinking of her own Christmas preparations. "What about my own family?" she thought. "My house isn't clean and I am having Christmas dinner."

Snowflakes were dancing overhead and everywhere, even the chalkboard. She smiled at the children who were so excited to see the snow. "Oh, how I wish I had your energy."

The class was eager to help with the old barn at the bottom of the box. Wooly sheep, brown camels, and donkeys were carefully unwrapped. Mary and Joseph were put on either side of the manger that the students filled with straw to cradle the Baby Jesus.

Blank white books were given to each child. Each boy or girl would be the author and illustrator of his or her very own Christmas story. These would be books to be shared every year with family and friends. An exhausted Mrs. Lee was starting a grand memory for the children!

Visions of the Christmas Programs, gifts for the children and letters to the homebound twirled in Mrs. Lee's mind. She also had to prepare the regular lessons and finish instruction for the class student's First Confession.

The students' attention span was getting shorter the closer they got to Christmas. They loved coloring and painting, but classroom assignments were becoming difficult to complete.

"The last day before Christmas vacation is one of the most challenging of all. To get work done, presents wrapped and the children safely home with all their gifts was a daunting task. And I still don't have any Christmas cards done!" confided the worried Mrs. Lee as the day approached. She was praying for a Christmas angel to intervene!

Dark clouds were building up in the sky. Gusty winds were blowing. A large storm was brewing as Mrs. Lee left for home.

During the night, the house shook with the storm, and ice formed interesting etchings on the windows. The teacher awoke at 5 am to go over her final checklist for school. The phone broke the early silence, "No school today because of the snow. Have a Merry Christmas!" the Principal said.

Mrs. Lee smiled. The projects could be sent home after Christmas. The party and program would be rescheduled. She could now begin preparing for her family's Christmas.

Her Christmas Angel had arrived!

*What we remember about Christmas depends upon a unique time and place.
Simple acts of love and acknowledgement transcend time and make the smallest
arrangements for a child live forever in her mind.*

MAMA'S TRUNK
BY CANDY BURKETT

I was barely five years old, the year was 1930. Mama had
said we were living in the "Great Depression," and though I
didn't understand what she meant, I knew there were times
when she was very sad. But suddenly it was Christmas and I
was bubbling all over with excitement of the holiday season.

I began to worry because we now lived in a small one
room apartment. I could not understand how Santa would
find me, as we had no chimney and no Christmas tree.
Mamma set me on her lap and said that Santa had all-seeing
eyes and since I was a very good little girl she was certain
that he would find me.

I bounced around the small room imaging what
Christmas morning would bring. When the magical day
finally arrived I looked around the room and saw no gifts,
and my heart fell. Mamma again sat me on her lap and said:
"Look around and see where Santa would have left a little
gift."

The room was very small and very bare but suddenly I
saw Mamma's old trunk at the foot of the bed. I slowly
opened it and Ho, Ho, Ho, Santa had found me after all.
There was one orange, an apple and a bag of mixed nuts, but
most of all a little Bylo baby doll that I would treasure for
years to come.

Now as my grandchildren gather around our Christmas
tree, I see their little faces all aglow with excitement. My
memories return to an old wooden trunk. To me it was more
beautiful than any decorated tree, for now I realize the love
that brought Santa to Mamma's trunk.

Want to know what it's really like to play Santa Claus? In this story, Don Hart draws on 15 years of personal experience "being the Man." At first, it is frightening. But as holiday seasons come and go, nothing seems more fulfilling than the delight on those wonderful, small faces. There's also some allegory buried in this Christmas story. Ever heard of a man named "Klaus from Myra?"

BELLS, WHISKERS & MAGIC
BY DON HART

His name was Klaus Myra and I heard later that he died on Christmas Day. I would not ordinarily have any interest in a guy like Klaus, but the boss insisted I visit him in the hospital and present him with a check from our corporation. One of the boss's charity deals. Myra was in charge of a Christian soup kitchen or something in the bad end of town.

When I went to see him he seemed upbeat for an old man who was supposed to be dying. He was bald and heavy, with very dark eyes, white hair and a beard. He looked Greek or Turkish and had very big hands. He obviously had broken his nose at sometime in his life, but seemed rather gentle for a brawler. It was odd that he could be friends with an august man like Rex J. Constantine III, my imperious boss. Mr. Constantine wanted me to be Santa Claus for his Children's Christmas Party that year, so he sent me to the Reverend Myra to ask him how to play it right and, well, get some training. I hated the whole idea. Since the old man was hospitalized, this seemed an impossible place to learn anything. But at least I could deliver the check.

"So Rex picked you to play Santa Claus this year?" he asked.

"Yeah, I don't know why."

"Well you got the build for it. You're not married are you? Would you like being Santa for little kids?"

"I guess so. Part of what I gotta do to get ahead at Roman Enterprises."

49

The old man let out a long ragged breath. He looked me over like Mr. Constantine's executives did when they were trying to size me up. They knew I had plenty of talent, but questioned whether I was the right man for advancement. I could tell this guy could have a hard edge if he wanted, but slowly he transformed and became a pleasant, loving sort of grandfather as he watched, and then said, "You'll do just fine, young man. It's all about bells, whiskers and magic. You know, I've been Santa Claus hundreds of times. It gets better every time you do it. That is, if you do it right."

"If I had whiskers like you have, it would probably be a lot easier."

"If you did Rex would probably fire you."

A chill ran through me. In those days my favorite movie was *Wall Street* and my favorite line was Michael Douglas playing Gordon Gekko and saying, "Greed is good." I was only doing this to please the big boss. My whole world was that nice corporate job I had with Roman. The old preacher seemed to pick up on my fear.

"What I mean is, your beard would be too dark. Children can't be afraid of you, because then you wouldn't really be Santa Claus. You have to think like you did when you were a small child."

The old man told me he had a good set of fake whiskers at his church along with a complete costume. He gave me the address and suggested I take the check to his assistant named Basil, who would suit me up for a trial appearance as Santa Claus at the church. After my debut, I was to come back for another visit so we could discuss my experience. This seemed like something Mr. Constantine would have set up, but I later learned the Reverend Myra had worked it all out himself.

I was with the old man less than five minutes the first

time. He said he was tired, looked at the clock and asked if I would leave and come back tomorrow.

***

When I got to the church and met his bedraggled assistant, I got the first of several surprises. The place was packed with desperate looking people who were being fed by religious workers in the church basement. Many people were asleep on the floor. The assistant named Brother Basil saw me coming and asked if I would give him the envelope right away and then he would be right back to help me. He tore it open quickly and pulled out a corporate check for $20,000 made out to Bishop Nicholas Myra. The assistant signed that name on the back right in front of me and disappeared into the crowd of wretches.

As I stood among the shabby people, dressed in my best suit of clothes, after the assistant fled, it seemed more than possible Mr. Constantine would fire me if that money vanished.

Children were crying and I heard people arguing. Then a priestly looking man appeared and asked me if I were there to help with Santa Claus. I followed him into an office where a table was neatly laid out with a red hat and costume, boots, whiskers, wig, large sleigh bells and a big red bag full of little wrapped gifts.

"Don't touch the bells till you get my signal," he said.

"What happened to Brother Basil?"

"He had to hurry to the bank. He'll be right back."

"Am I supposed to be Santa Claus today?"

"Sure, at 2:00 o'clock. Didn't the Bishop tell you?"

"I didn't even know he was a bishop. No, he just said you would show me the costume."

"Bishop Myra has many other churches. Since he can't do it this year, he might want you to be Santa at the other missions."

This thing had gone way too far. I noticed the phone on the big desk and asked if I could call my office. When Mr. Constantine answered he told me to just do what Brother Basil asked and don't worry about his check. He wanted me to get all the Santa Claus training I could from Klaus Myra.

"Don't worry about showing up to work until the Company Christmas Party tomorrow night. Then be ready to play Santa for the employees' kids. Klaus told me you will do just fine and that you can use his costume."

I put down the phone and stood in shock.

"The most important part of playing Santa, the Bishop always says, is getting the whiskers right," said the priest.

"Yeah, but his whiskers are always right, *on him*," I said, trying to recover.

"Here let's get yours fitted perfect."

Then the priest put the beard over my face and tightened the elastic several places on the back and top of my head. The thing started itching immediately. He helped me on with the wig and put the red hat on top. I looked in the mirror. It was astounding!

"Best set of whiskers money can buy," said Brother Basil, rushing back into the office. "That's the key to making this work. Of course, the bells and magic are mighty important too."

The two men laughed at each other like old friends enjoying the same good joke over and over again.

Before long I was dressed in the red suit, with boots and buckle just right. I looked in a full-length mirror. The two religious men knew just what they were doing. They had been "Santa valets" to the Bishop for years and enjoyed it immensely.

"Only when I give the signal, you grab the big sleigh bells and start ringing them all the way out to the kids. Then, sit down in the Santa chair we have for you in the corner out there and just be Santa Claus," said Brother Basil.

"But, I don't know what to do!"

"Do like the Bishop does. Be gentle, ask 'em if they been good; ask what they want for Christmas; give them a little gift from the bag, and then go to the next kid. When you're done, ring your bells and come back in here."

"I don't know if I can remember all that."

"Just act like you're Santa. It'll all work out. Now Father John is going out to get all the kids ready and start them singing. I'll give you a signal when to come out," said Basil. Then both men disappeared.

I waited in trepidation wondering if I could pull this off. The beard was really itching. I wondered if someone would steal my suit, or maybe my car, while I was occupied with this project.

Then I heard children laughing and singing. The atmosphere in the church was changing. It was now beginning to be alive and exciting. I could not see the people, but I began to feel the magic. Things got quiet, jovial and prayerful all at once.

"Show time," said Brother Basil. "As soon as the kids start singing Jingle Bells, come on out."

I came out terrified. All the people were staring at me in anticipation. It was quiet. Then, I rang the bells and roared, "HO, HO, HO, MERRY CHRISTMAS!"

The magic began.

Soon the children came up one by one and poured out their hearts. "Yes, I been good." "I want a Barbie Doll and a gurgle%gugla with stars on it, etc." Half the time I couldn't make out what they were saying. Then I gave them a little present. Some kids were suspicious I might take it back. Then they would leave happy and another kid would come up and sit on my lap. "I been good, but my brother Willie has been real bad." "I want a puppy and also a fijlefrabusball." "Could you give me a kubblebonorie this year?" "We had to move to Aunt Freddie's, do you know where she lives?"

Some kids would not sit on my lap for all the candy in Canada. Others would jump right up and hug me tight. Adorable little faces, full of hope, fear, joy and fun. There was skepticism and wonder. "Where are your reindeer?" "I want for Christmas...Oh, I forgot." Beautiful children already showing adult charm in their faces. Incredibly heavy children, who do not appear fat. Children with raggedy clothes and dirty nails. Children with frightened, haunted looks. Children exceptionally clean with wide, beautiful eyes. "I want, ah, I want my daddy to come out of jail." "Thank you, Santa Claus!"

In a few minutes, it was all over.

"Santa has to get back to the North Pole, now," said Father John.

Then, I got up out of the chair and started ringing the big sleigh bells.

"Everyone keep being good now," I said, and then I headed back to the office and closed the door. As soon as I was out of sight, I ripped off my beard and scratched my itchy face. But, I think it went OK. So did the Bishop's assistant.

"Well, are you ready to do St. Paul's at 4 o'clock?" asked Brother Basil.

As I drove to St. Paul's, Basil told me about Klaus Myra. He was originally from Greece or Turkey and lost his parents who died in a plague when he was young. They were very wealthy and very religious. When he was old enough to get his inheritance, he gave all of it away to poor people and tried to become a priest, but he was too young, so he signed on a ship to sail to America. His ship almost sank in a storm crossing over and he saved several sailors from drowning. When he prayed for the storm to quit, it quit immediately, and all his shipmates thought he had managed a miracle. In America, his reputation for serendipity was everywhere. Helping people in trouble got him into the religious life and he became a bishop at a young age.

"Bishop Klaus is the greatest Santa I've ever seen," said Basil. "He can teach you some good things. Long ago, someone gave him a white horse he rode as Santa from church to church. Told the kids he liked it better than reindeer and a sleigh when there was no snow on the ground. He looked great on top of that horse at Christmas time and really loved it. But he only had it a short while. We found out he got a good offer on the horse and sold it, so he could feed more poor people and keep them warm in church."

At St. Paul's and later at St. Philip's and two other churches the next day, I got more experience with the children and some of their parents. I learned to be careful answering questions and dealing with crazy Christmas wishes.

"How old are you? Mother says you're older than a hundred. Are you?" "Do your reindeer have babies? Can the babies fly too?" "How many elves do you have? Do they make Barbie Doll clothes?" "We don't have a chimney where

I live. How you gonna bring me anything?" "Can you get a two-wheel-bike down the chimney?"

The parents' questions could be worse. "Santa, did you tell her she could have a kitten? We can't have a live cat in our family! Hell, we can't even feed ourselves." "You didn't promise her that? You didn't? Susan, how would you like Santa to give you a darn good spanking?"

On the afternoon before the company Christmas party, I met with Klaus again for the last time. I told him everything I've told you and he was most pleased. He wanted me to have his costume and his wonderful big sleigh bells. I agreed to take the stuff, *"only if you can't do Santa yourself* next year."

He reminded me that each child is different and faces Santa with different motives and anxieties, so kindness and patience are very important. He told me not to let adults force the "scaredy cats." Also, that children remember their experience with Santa Claus long after childhood. Then we got into the area of belief.

"Be careful not to do anything that will destroy a child's belief," he warned me. "It's important to keep up the loving magic until the child learns to make his own. At that point, the boy or girl understands what it means to bring joy and charity to other people."

"How does that work?" I asked him.

"It works because simple giving provides more than the gift itself. If it shows personal care to the individual, a spiritual need is also filled. A little heart needs individual attention as much as the heavy heart of an old person."

On the night of the company Christmas party I felt the confidence that Klaus gave me. The affluent children were different only in the gifts they expected: electronic gizmos and the latest whiz-bangs. The children all had those same wonderful faces and wide eyes. Some of them got around a little more than children from the shelter:

"What do you want for Christmas?"

"I told you at the mall."

These children had to have their pictures taken more often because their parents had nice cameras. I learned to gently take the children's' hands away from their mouths and have them say "Merry Christmas, everybody" while the picture is shot. That's probably how I caught a cold the next day, but the pictures turned out great.

Another thing. Any intelligent baby is going to be afraid of a grizzly old man in a strange red outfit 50 times the size of an infant. If you want a good picture, set up your camera for an immediate take right after you place the child on Santa's lap. Keep their backs to Santa so the baby can't see Santa before she is placed in his lap. You will only have about 4 seconds. If your baby sees Santa too early, and gets frightened, you will have 0 seconds to get a good picture.

I left Roman Enterprises and Mr. Constantine's employ a few years later. It has been nice to leave the rat race and do a job where I can be more like Klaus and less like Rex. Every Christmas since, I have volunteered at the churches to be their Santa Claus. Now I am old. I grow my own whiskers, and my beard is as white as my hair. I still have Klaus' big set of sleigh bells that ring so clear they cheer people up from a block away.

But, best of all, Bishop Klaus gave me that individual gift I needed to make life more fulfilling. From long ago, when I was moving in the direction of emptiness, he has shown me the promise of our beautiful children and the magic of Christmas.

Santa's life is not always joyful. He takes on enormous responsibilities in attempting to satisfy the many children who depend on him. The author has spent over 35 years helping continue the magic of the Christmas holiday by visiting children in their homes. Now and then he gets a request that is hard to fulfill.

A SPECIAL CHRISTMAS WISH
BY D. A. QUIGLEY

"Santa, is that you?" someone called out.

The surprise question startled him. It was a cold December night with temperatures continuing to drop and Santa was in a hurry to get to his sleigh. He just wanted to return as quickly as possible to the comfort of his North Pole. He was out of breath and could not see very well through his white hair hanging out from under his red stocking cap. His wire-rimmed glasses, fogged from running through backyards, were now sitting at the end of his nose. Besides the cold, it was snowing with light, confetti-sized snowflakes softy covering everything. The only light came from a single lamp post at the end of a tree-lined cul-de-sac. The leaves on the trees had long disappeared. He had finished his visit to a Christmas display, inconspicuously vanished from the scene and was headed back to his sleigh. He had not been as fast as his elf. He was already standing by the sleigh ready to take off.

After adjusting his glasses and looking around, he saw the source of the voice. A woman was standing on the front steps of the house across the street and she was waving at him. He waved to her.

"HO, HO, HO, Merry Christmas!" he called back to her, turning to continue his walk towards the waiting sleigh.

Then he heard the voices of little children. They had joined the woman on the front porch.

59

"Santa...Santa is that you? Are you coming to my house tonight?" a little girl shouted.

Santa stopped in his tracks, turned and looked at the children. Hesitating for only a moment, he headed across the street. He could not disappoint any little children. In accepting his role to visit young children and listen to their special wishes, Santa took his responsibility seriously.

Santa was immediately ushered inside. There were a number of families gathered. All the children quickly found their way to the foyer to greet him. At first he stood by the staircase leading to a second floor. He had just walked through a number of backyards and his boots were wet with snow and caked with dirt from not quite frozen flower beds. Reluctant to venture past the foyer for fear of staining the white carpet, he stayed put. After a few minutes greeting the children, he sat down on one of the steps and all the children had their turn sitting on his lap, with the exception of a little girl who stood by his side patiently waiting for her turn. She and her brother were the little children from the front porch who invited him into the house.

She was a lovely little girl with curly shoulder length blond hair. She was picture perfect dressed in a red satin dress with a pink sash around her waist. Santa could tell she was shy and apprehensive by the way she played with the ruffled sleeves of her dress. When she finally had her turn she pointed out her new black ballet slippers and white tights which she said made her feel very grown up. She indicated that her little brother, Daniel, who was only three years old, was afraid of Santa. When Santa looked in Daniel's direction he could tell she was right by the death grip he had on his mother's leg. They were both standing by the entrance to the kitchen, mother with a camera in hand, waiting to snap a perfect picture of her daughter sitting on Santa's lap, while her son clung for dear life.

"What is your name?" Santa asked.

"Jennifer, and I am five years old," she told Santa. As was his custom with all children, regardless of their age, he continued, asking the usual question.

"What do you want Santa to bring you for Christmas?"

Jennifer's was not the usual answer. As innocent as she could be and with a little crack in her tender voice, she asked Santa for something he knew he could not deliver. Instead of the toys, games or baby dolls that most children ask for at her age, she asked for something very special.

"Santa can you make my daddy walk again?"

Santa was speechless. He could not respond with his customary, "Yes, my elves are busy making lots of them this year."

Since Santa delayed somewhat in answering, Jennifer turned her head and looked straight into his eyes. He would have to come up with something.

"That was a very special request and Santa will do his best to make you happy!" he finally said.

Jennifer gave him a big hug, jumped down, and joined her brother at her mother's side.

Before Santa left the house, he circulated among the families and was introduced to all gathered there for the evening. At the end of the dining room table sat a man in a wheelchair. Jennifer went over to his side. Daniel and his mother were standing behind the wheelchair. When Santa was introduced, the man smiled and gave a short wave moving his mouth to say, "Thank You!" Santa waved back, nodding his head in reply.

Santa left the house with a lasting memory of Jennifer and her wish. He was deeply saddened with the knowledge that he could not deliver that special Christmas wish for Jennifer.

***

The following June, I found myself thinking about Jennifer and her request. I remembered that snowy night and how Santa was speechless in responding to the little girl's wish. What could Santa have done differently? Could he have said something different? These and similar questions dominated my thoughts while standing in line at the Harris Bank branch one Saturday morning. After leaving the bank, I made up my mind to revisit that neighborhood again and search for Jennifer and her family.

I found the neighborhood with no problem. Since it was now summertime, I did not have to worry about people recognizing me out of my magical suit. As I drove around in search of the street and cul-de-sac where Santa had parked his sleigh that snowy night the previous December, the landscape looked quite different. The trees were in full bloom and green lawns replaced the snow-covered ground. Before long I found the street and recognized the house where the lady had called out Santa's name.

Going up to the house, I was a bit nervous since I knew that the person who answered the door would not recognize me. I paused for a moment before pressing the door bell. An attractive woman and a young child answered the door. I introduced myself to the woman and told her that I was searching for the little girl who had made the special request to Santa the previous Christmas. At first it did not register with her who I was. Then gradually the quizzical look on her face began to change as she became aware of who I must be. After giving me a hug and thanking me, she was excited to tell me Jennifer's story and provide the background information that led up to that night. She was very pleased that I had returned to find Jennifer and her family. The neighbors and Jennifer's parents had often talked about whether they would ever get to meet the Santa who was walking down the street that cold December night that they were having their party.

The party had been a special celebration, not only for Christmas, but also a welcome home party for Jennifer's dad. Two weeks earlier, on the night before Thanksgiving, he had been in a serious car accident. A drunk driver ran a red light. The accident happened two miles from Jennifer's house. After being hospitalized and told he would never walk again, he returned to his home. The accident had a devastating effect on his family, especially Jennifer. She had always been an active, cheerful little girl, the first to greet her daddy when he entered the house each night after work.

After the accident, Jennifer became reclusive and very quiet. That is, until she saw Santa that snowy night while looking out the front window of the house where the party was being held. When she happened to see me walking down the street, she shouted Santa's name and ran to the front door in hopes he was coming to visit her. She secretly wished that he was coming to answer her silent prayer. Until that night when she sat on Santa's lap and asked for her special wish, she had not spoken a single word about the accident or the fact that her father was confined to a wheelchair. After Santa left she finally spent time with her father, often explaining how the magical man in the red suit and white beard was going to grant her wish. She truly believed in his magic.

***

Jennifer's home was only a short distance down the street from where this woman lived. Leaving my car parked in front of her home, I did not have far to walk. As I approached the house, I could still see Jennifer sitting on Santa's lap six months earlier. My mind tried to imagine what might have happened to the family since that night. How had they adjusted to the new circumstances that life had dealt them? Did Jennifer still believe in Santa even though he had not fulfilled her wish?

Standing on the front porch I could hear classical piano music coming from inside. The melody of Rachmaninoff's "Rhapsody on a Theme of Paganini" brought a smile to my face. How ironic it was that the score from the movie, "Somewhere in Time" should be playing at that moment. It lifted my spirit as I pressed the door bell twice hoping someone would be able to hear the chimes over the music. I didn't have to wait long before I heard a man's voice.

"Come in!" a male voice shouted.

"Where did that come from?" I asked myself, stepping back from the door to see if a downstairs window was open. Or was it coming from a neighbor?

I realized the voice was coming from a window above me. I apprehensively opened the front door and stepped inside, initially not seeing the person who had invited me into the house.

"Hello, may I help you?" The voice came from the top of the L shaped stairs which led to a landing on the second floor.

Looking up, I saw a slender man wearing glasses with a curious look on his face sitting in a wheelchair at the top of the steps. Even though I recognized the gentleman as Jennifer's father, he had no idea that he was looking at Santa since I was in street clothes. It was understandable.

I quickly introduced myself and asked if he was Jennifer's father, just to make sure. His look of curiosity quickly changed to one of concern and his voice grew in intensity.

"Yes, why are you asking?" he asked.

I began recounting my version of the story of what had happened the previous December when I was asked to come into his neighbor's home as Santa. His facial expression went from one of concern to a wide smile. He interrupted, asking me to join him in his new upstairs office.

As I reached the top of the staircase, he greeted me but not with a customary handshake. He insisted on giving me a big hug, which made the moment particularly emotional. He invited me to sit in his office, which overlooked his beautifully landscaped backyard and several of his neighbors'. They were the same yards that Santa had used as a short cut, minus the snow and dirt!

Jennifer's dad explained that his company made arrangements for him to work from home while he was recuperating. Since he was an architect and engineer he could work easily away from the office. When he looked up from his work, he got to watch the neighborhood children playing in the backyards. The family had remodeled their home, installing an elevator in the back of the house where there had originally been a second staircase.

Jennifer's dad was delighted to meet Santa again. He was obviously dressed differently than when we first met but then, so was I. His suit had been replaced with a pair of warm-up pants and a golf shirt. The car accident had taken a toll on his body but not his spirit. His smile told me that. He was no longer the athlete who had competed in a marathon two years before, but his energy and positive spirit had increased over time. He thanked me for having changed the lives of his family. He said the night his daughter talked with Santa brought them back together again.

We discussed that December night when Jennifer made her surprising wish and how ironic and coincidental that Santa just happened to be in the neighborhood that night. I told Jennifer's father that I wanted to do something special for his daughter. He suggested that I arrange for Santa to visit again the following December on that same weekend two weeks before Christmas. With a sly grin I told him that it could be easily arranged. I provided him the secret phone number for my North Pole and asked him to contact Mrs. Claus so they could make arrangements on Santa's busy schedule.

December came in a flash and I visited Jennifer's house one Saturday night, a week before Christmas. Many of her relatives, close friends and neighbors were there, including the family whose home Santa had visited the year before.

I rang the door bell and Daniel answered with Jennifer close behind. Her little brother was no longer shy or afraid to speak with Santa. He wasted no time in telling Santa what was on his list.

The family gathered in the great room in the rear of the house in front of the fireplace which had a beautiful Christmas wreath hanging above the mantel. They placed a comfortable chair near the fireplace and asked Santa to sit there while Jennifer's brother discussed his wish list. Soon it was Jennifer's turn to visit with Santa. She was one year older but her innocence and charm had not changed. She pointed out to everyone that Santa was still wearing the same boots, the same white gloves with red stains and ringing the same sleigh bells that he had the year before.

"This must be the real Santa! My friends will be so jealous!" she proclaimed to everyone in the room.

Jennifer began by thanking me for coming back to visit her again. I was careful about how I answered her compliment.

"You are a special little girl" I told her. "Santa cannot make all dreams come true every year, but he can bring lots of joy to everyone in different ways!"

Jennifer smiled and gave Santa a big hug. Then, I spent time with others at the party. There were many photos and movies taken to remember the occasion.

***

Jennifer's story was special. It involved some unforeseen circumstances. Jennifer just happened to be looking out the front window of the neighbor's house when she saw Santa walking down the street that night. Santa's unscheduled visit with her and her family taught him an important lesson that not all of Santa's gifts have to be in neatly wrapped packages placed under a tree. He had not been able to fulfill Jennifer's first wish, but that did not mean that she and her family hadn't received a precious gift.

Don't be disappointed when you don't see all the gifts you ask for under the tree on Christmas morning; sometimes the gift is there but you cannot see it. In my case it was a lump of coal, which was a special gift my parents provided to me when I was young. The best gifts are the ones wrapped in love.

This poem is an introduction to the story The Candy Castle in this anthology. What makes a great story is when you can really "put yourself into it." Same for a child. They will even get to decide their role in the enchantment to come. Save this story and try reading it to a group of children. (Be sure to keep their names straight.)

ON MARY LOU'S LAP
BY MARY LOU MCCARTHY

*At my Grandma's house
One Christmas Eve
The ground was covered in snow.
My sister and I
Sit in our room,
Trying to pass the time.
We run to the adults.
"Mary Lou! Mary Lou!"
"Tell us a story!"
She would always say yes,
And scoop us up on her lap.
The story was called
"The Candy Castle"
Of two beautiful princesses
Named after my sister and me.
We were entranced by the story
Of witches and magic.
She told it so well.
And even today,
As I am older,
I will always remember sitting
On Mary Lou's lap.*

THE CANDY CASTLE
(ADAPTABLE CHILDREN'S STORY)
BY MARY LOU MCCARTHY

Chapter 1—A Castle Made of Candy

Once upon a time, in a land far away, there was an enchanted castle ... a magic castle ... a castle that was made entirely of candy.

So, of course, it was called the Candy Castle, and everything about it was sweet.

The bricks were giant Brownies...

The castle door was made of licorice.

And all the windows were trimmed with chocolate drops. Rain and snow couldn't harm the castle, and even the summer sun could not melt the chocolate drops!

High on the roof, there was a rampart of candy bars, where the guards kept watch.

They had to be on guard, because everyone wanted a bite of the Candy Castle.

Chapter 2—The Royal Family

A royal family lived in the castle, headed by King ____ the Wise, Queen ____ the Lovely, Prince ____ the Smart and Princess ____ the Sweet.

The King and Queen were always about their royal duties, running the Candy Kingdom, keeping it good and fair, just and kind.

That left the Prince and Princess free to explore and discover. Of course, there were dozens of governesses, gardeners and guards to watch over them, ensuring they didn't stray too far or break too many rules.

One day, the royal cousins, Prince _____ and Princess _____, came to visit. "This is great!" exclaimed Prince ____. "We are off on an adventure!"

The four cousins jumped on their magic ponies and off they galloped, into the Candy Kingdom.

Chapter 3—The Attack of the Wicked Pirates

The cousins rode ponies that were magical indeed. Each cousin had a magic word, and when the pony heard it, the pony and rider would disappear! They could be felt and heard, but not seen. This fact was very important on that special afternoon.

Prince _____, the oldest cousin, named his black pony _____, and Prince _____ named his pony_____, while Princess_____ named her multicolored pony _____ and her young Princess cousin called hers _____.

As they were riding along the coast, they heard men's voices and the lapping of oars. "It's the Pirates!" exclaimed Prince_____. "Use your magic word and disappear!" Instantly, they vanished. They saw a gang of fierce-looking pirates landing on the shore, and heard their evil plan... "Now we can capture the Candy Castle and all its riches!"

The cousins galloped like the wind to warn the Candy Castle.

"What?" exclaimed King _____. "Pirates? No way!"

"You children have such imaginations!" said Queen _____. "Now shoo. We've very busy today. Why don't you keep watch for the pirates up in the tower?"

Up in the tower, they watched until dark, then they got tired and it was time for supper and bed. But in the middle of the night, they awoke to a great commotion.

The cousins snuck out of their bedrooms and just as they predicted, Pirates were robbing the castle. The Pirates even had the King and Queen tied up. "Where have you hidden the treasure?" they threatened.

"I have an idea," whispered Prince _____. "Follow me down the secret passage to the laboratory."

In the lab, Prince _____ looked up the formula for Fool's Gold, and they set about making a bag full of gold coins to trap the Pirates. When they were done, they dropped a path of coins right out the door and into the guardhouse, which they disguised as a treasure house.

Once the trap was set, they sent the family dog _____ into the room. _____ barked and sniffed a coin on the floor, and a Pirate said, "Look at the dog—he's onto something gold!"

The plan worked like clockwork. The Pirates followed the trail of Fool's Gold, and when the last one was in the guardhouse, the kids slammed the door and locked it tight.

The Pirates were tried and punished for their deeds, and after they were released, they were paroled into the Kingdom of Candy. Over time, they came to love it and settled down to become law-abiding citizens!

King _____ and Queen _____ complimented the children for their cleverness and awarded them with the Medal of Honor for protecting the Candy Castle.

A lovely thing about Christmas is its certainty. It comes around yearly whether we are ready or not. Its traditions and rituals are reliable too. This story reminds us how important these become in the mind of a child, even many years after they are faithfully performed.

CHRISTMAS EVE AT THE CHURCH OF THE MASTER
BY PRISCILLA MUTTER

The church of my childhood was a small white church, like a thousand other little country churches. It was not affiliated with any particular denomination, just a small country church of simple farmers.

My favorite part of our religious tradition was our Christmas Eve service. It never varied in any way from year to year. First, the choir would march up the aisles singing "O Come All Ye Faithful." Our minister would read the account of the birth of Christ from the scriptures. And then the kids would perform.

My Aunt Annette was the Sunday School director. She gave us poems to memorize; this was called "saying a piece." The length of the piece was based on your age and memorization skills. The boys were given shorter poems because they were thought to be poorer at memorizing, and as I remember, they were, or maybe not, as motivated as the girls.

The boys were embarrassed and self-conscious, and said their pieces with red faces and agonized body language. Sometimes they forgot their pieces and my aunt would help them by loudly whispering their lines.

The children would sing solos, and sometimes duets. One year I sang "It Came Upon the Midnight Clear" with my cousin, who could read music, and we managed shaky two-part harmony. My Aunt Annette would always do a dramatic reading with arm gestures and a tremulous voice, usually something containing "Behold! There is a star in the East!"

The second best part was when the little girls would sit on the steps leading to the pulpit with their baby dolls, and sing "Away in a Manger" while rocking their dolls in their arms. Not a dry eye in the house.

Then, the best part. We would finish, of course, with "Silent Night." Our minister would say a benediction and then, "Wait! What's that I hear?" and we would listen. Sleigh bells, outside our church door!

In would bustle Santa, our good-natured neighbor, Theron Smith. Theron was tall and stringy, an unlikely Santa, but he was good at it, willing, and he did it every year. He had a shabby Santa suit and a ratty ragged beard. The buckle on his phony patent leather belt peeled away a little more leather every year. He would move up the aisles, stopping to talk to the little kids in the pews with their parents. They sat absolutely still, thrilled and terrified, their eyes huge, and sometimes they would bury their faces in their dads' necks.

Santa would talk to the kids, and, from his pillow case of gifts, give each child wrapped taffy in animal cracker-like boxes. He would wish all of us a very Merry Christmas and then, saying that he had to get busy delivering toys, noisily Ho-Ho-Ho back out the door, into the night.

The silence was broken. An excited din followed. Santa had been here! He had given the kids candy! And he would be coming to their houses later tonight with toys! The country people talked together for a while, and then went out into the night to go home and wait for the excitement of the big day.

Sometimes around Christmas good plans can go really awry. This story is a fictional example of just how far awry things can go.

ALMOST TOO LATE
BY DON PEACOCK

It was 8:00 pm on Christmas Eve. Phil was all alone in his living room. His wife was upstairs in bed sound asleep, which was a good indicator of the type of day she had had.

"Thank goodness I've got that all finished," he thought. "I've bought something for everyone on the list plus a couple of extras they won't suspect they are getting. I played it smart and got everything wrapped at the stores and hidden where they can't be found. Now I can lean back and relax for the rest of this Christmas Eve."

With that he kicked back, popped open a Dos Equis beer, put his feet up and prepared to relax and watch his favorite shows for the evening. He picked up the remote and turned on TCM channel to watch the 1936 black and white movie "San Francisco." About a third of the way into the movie he started to doze off when his eyes suddenly snapped open, a horrified look appeared on his face, his mouth flew open and out came, "Oh my gosh, she wanted that diamond pendant and I only have the CD player and the new ironing board for her now. How could I have forgotten that even in all of the hustle and bustle of the season?"

With that he rose to his feet, fired out the door, jumped into his car and took off for the mall, which, obviously, turned out to be mobbed with all of the procrastinators and others who had not thought it out too well. It took him over fifteen minutes to find a parking place. He then hurriedly made his way to a still open jewelry store while trying not to bump into too many people since most of them were also highly agitated about not having finished their Christmas shopping.

When he finally got to the store, he was told to take a number and wait for it to be called. He pulled out the next number, 97, just as the call came out, "Now serving number 63."

"Oh my God" was the first thing out of his mouth. The next was "You have got to be kidding me." He quickly ran through thoughts on (1) going elsewhere (same crowded problem), (2) giving her a note saying the pendant would come next week (he was dead if he did this), and (3) giving up and going back home without the pendant (he would be even deader and never would hear the end of it.). He knew his only option was to stay and wait, no matter how long it took. And it did take a long time. It seemed to Phil like one hundred years, but finally at ten minutes to midnight, which was the store's special closing hour for Christmas eve, Phil was the next to last customer left in the store. The clerks were definitely not in the Christmas mood by this time and Phil was not in any better mood than they were. In fact he was probably in an even worse mood, if that were possible. When they finally called, "Number 97, please," Phil went over to the clerk and said that he wanted to buy a diamond pendant, about a quarter carat or slightly smaller.

The clerk's responded, "We only have three left and only one less than half a carat."

Phil looked at all three and asked, "Are you sure you don't have any others left in the back of the store?"

"If we had any more they would be out here because they have sold like wildfire. These are the only choices you have, unless you want to go searching for another store in town that is still open."

Phil finally chose the middle sized one. It was a little bit more than he wanted to pay but it was the nicest one, so he pulled out his charge card and paid for the transaction. He then asked, "Do you Christmas wrap?" The clerk tried not to sneer but couldn't suppress it.

"Christmas wrap! At this hour! Are you insane? I'm locking up in five minutes and going home to have several Margaritas."

"Where else can I get this wrapped?" Phil pleaded.

"How about at your place?" the clerk responded, her voice getting louder. "Try it you might like it." With that she semi-gently pushed him to the door and out into the mall, locked the door and started into her closing procedure. All the time she was mumbling, "Christmas, bah humbug. Christmas, bah humbug. I have to find a better job before next year."

Phil went out to his car, jumped in, and started down the street looking for an open drug store since they always seemed to have plenty of leftover Christmas stuff like wrapping paper, ribbon, and bows. By the time he got to the third drugstore trying to find what he needed, he was sweating blood and in a total panic. Charging in, he asked, louder than he should have, "Lord, I hope you have some wrapping materials left. I don't care what they look like. I need them. NOW!!"

"Certainly. All of our Christmas stuff is in aisle seven, over to the left. Get whatever you need. It's all that we have left." Phil charged over to aisle seven, looked and groaned. It was some of the ugliest paper, ribbon and bows he had ever seen.

"Now I know why they have it left on the shelf," he remarked. "Newspaper would make better wrapping paper then this stuff." Still he bought what he needed, paid for it and headed back to his car. On his drive home he kept telling himself to make notes in the future to avoid this ever happening again.

When he finally got home he grabbed all the stuff he had bought, hurried into the house and laid it all on the table. Luckily, his wife was still in bed sound asleep. Hurriedly he wrapped the pendant, doing the typically male job of it. It looked like it was wrapped in the middle of an evacuation for a hurricane plus the color of the bow was a total mismatch, but the important thing was it was wrapped. He quickly placed it under the tree and went over to sit on the sofa in front of the TV. It was 4:00 am and he had made it. He lay down on the sofa to relax. The next thing he knew it was 6:00 am. Just then his wife came down the stairs stretching and yawning. She came over to him and commented. "I'm sorry. I'm afraid I went out like a light last night. I'm just glad that we got all of our shopping done early enough so we both could get a good night's sleep." Then, noticing his rumpled clothes, she asked "Hey, have you been sitting in front of the TV all night?"

"Yes, I have. I had a couple of Dos Equis and fell asleep on the sofa. I slept like a log. Let's go open our presents."

MEMORIES OF CHRISTMASES PAST
BY PAT AND BOB (HUTCH) O'CONNOR
(AKA THE CLAUSES)

1963—1965, DeKalb, Illinois

We were living in a small rental house with five children under the age of six! Kennedy had been assassinated in November 1963. We had just moved to this little Illinois town since I had accepted a position of Personnel Director with a large manufacturing company. Both of our families were hundreds of miles away. The Sunday before Christmas a Santa appeared at our door with gifts for each of our children. To this day we have no idea who this Santa really was. Pat was so impressed with the joy he brought our entire family that the next year she made a beautiful Santa outfit and thus began a journey of over 46 years of *Santa Clausing*.

1966—1969, Chicago and the Suburbs

I had taken a new position of Director of Industrial Relations with a company owned by Sears and we moved into the suburb of Elk Grove Village. Continued our Santa Claus visits to neighbors, kindergartens, etc. But we had a much different reception than we experienced in the little town of DeKalb. People were much more cautious in welcoming us to their homes. Before in DeKalb, I would knock on the doors of neighbors, and the family would simply open their door, and we would place candy canes in the hands of the children and move on. Guess the big city syndrome (of being cautious when strangers knock on your door) prevailed.

1969—present, Dayton, Ohio

In early 1969 I accepted the position of Manager of Labor Relations for the marketing division of NCR. The very first Christmas, a manager in our office asked if I would visit his mom in a Washington Manor Nursing Home as Santa. (He said the Santa they originally had was not very good!)

Pat decided she would enjoy playing Mrs. Claus—she is an accomplished seamstress and made a very attractive Mrs. Claus suit.

We had a fabulous time attending this nursing home's Christmas Party—family and friends of the residents all gathered in the large dinning room and each old person received a gift from Santa. Since this was the very first time we visited this nursing home as The Clauses it was quite a well received event. But on the way home that evening Pat said to me, "Bob, I do not think I will play Mrs. Claus any more!" Shocked, I inquired why. She replied that several old men residents pinched her on her bottom! We laughed and I simply said, "Heck, Mrs. Claus, wear tight jeans under your outfit in the future!" She did so from that Christmas forward!

Oh, another thing happened there—we had our son and some of his OSU band members play Script Ohio and a very old resident stopped us and said, "Do you know I ran the very first touchdown in OSU Horse Shoe stadium in 1921?" His wife told him he shouldn't be bragging, but we are glad he did. Sadly, he was not there the following year.

As the years followed, we volunteered our services to many nursing homes, retirement villages, Head Start programs, Christmas gatherings at churches, and for our neighbors and friends' families. Some of our more memorable experiences follow.

<u>Nursing Homes</u>—when Brighton Gardens came to town we were asked to visit there—this is a very plush retirement facility, built and run by the Marriott out of Washington, DC. Each year they would have us visit and have candy canes for each of their residents—who would sit on our laps—the men on Mrs. Claus and women on Santa's.

The third year of making our trips to Brighton Gardens we were asked if we would visit the Alzheimer's unit. Naturally we readily agreed and the attendant unlocked a door that led into that unit. Mrs. Claus immediately spied several women sort of staring off into space. We decided to give each one a candy cane. I spotted one little old lady, all by herself, standing in a corner. I approached her saying, "Hey, honey, all my life I wanted to give you a special Christmas candy cane." Her quick response was, "You old SOB. I always did hate you!" (So much for my Irish charm.)

A nurse told me later not to be offended. This woman thought I was her husband dressed as Santa!

Head Starts—We made scheduled appearances at several Head Start facilities, e.g., downtown Dayton, Miamisburg and elsewhere. One snowy Wednesday afternoon, just before Christmas, I was dressed in my Santa outfit and sipping a cup of coffee at my kitchen table waiting for Mrs. Claus when the phone rang.

The voice said, "This is Dorothy at Head Start. Where is Santa Claus?" (My wife had informed me we were to visit Pratt School's kindergarten at 10:00 am that day. Mrs. Claus is in charge of scheduling and posts our calendar of visits starting as early as September—remember we normally make between 25 and 35 visits each holiday season.)

When I questioned Pat, AKA Mrs. Santa, she replied: "Head Start is on the schedule for Thursday, tomorrow, and Pratt is today!"

I passed that message on to Dorothy who responded, "Oh we will not be here tomorrow. You will terribly disappoint twelve little kids!"

Well, I tried to explain that we were previously scheduled. But as I watched the soft snow falling on our way to Pratt School and I began to think maybe, just maybe, Pat had messed up the days. When we arrived at Pratt, I suggested she check with the principal. A few minutes later she came running out to the car and said nervously—"I made a mistake Pratt is tomorrow!" Well we were about a half hour from the Head Start location, and rushed there appearing shortly before lunch. Our visit was to be held in the basement of a church. We went down the steps to find twelve little children in a circle singing Christmas songs. I got down with them and asked if they knew we were coming. They replied, "Our teacher mentioned you may not make it. We asked what should we do, and she told us to 'Pray for a Miracle!' "

Enable Industries Ogden, Utah 2001

Our oldest son, Kevin, was Vice President of a manufacturing firm, IOMEGA, in Ogden. They subcontracted some of their light assembling tasks to Enable Industries—a firm that employed all types of handicapped people. He had flown us out to Utah to play the Clauses at several of his company's Christmas parties and scheduled our appearance at Enable Industries.

As we entered the assembling floor we were immediately greeted by a large number of mentally and physically handicapped workers. The smile on their faces showed true, unadulterated joy at our visit. We had special large candy canes for each. You would not believe the sincerity of thanks we received—many hugging us in appreciation! We visited one area where a man with no hands was filling cartons with his feet. He seemed mildly embarrassed until a co-worker brought him to us to receive his candy cane. The thing we remember most was entering a room where the most severely handicapped workers were—all had on helmets to protect their heads. Their smiles were more than enough reward for us!

Inner City Schools of Dayton

Since two of our grandchildren, now both in college, had attended Holy Family, an inner city school, as grade school kids, we asked if they might accompany us, returning as Santa's elves. They were somewhat reluctant, but quickly

84

took on the task. Kids from kindergarten to third grade gathered at the feet of the Clauses to hear the Christmas Story. We always begin with a question, "What can you give your mom, dad, brothers, sisters, and grandparents that does not cost ANY money?"

Each child that answered correctly received a special gift. Wonderfully, many responded correctly: "LOVE, KISSES, AND HUGS."

Once, when Mrs. Claus made a comment to the fourth graders that we were late because "Rudolph broke his leg," one girl responded harshly. She said, "Mrs. Claus, that is very irresponsible of you! You should have told the *Dayton Daily News* so we could all know about it." Mrs. Claus immediately replied, "Oh, but Children's Hospital set the leg immediately so Rudolph could help pull Santa's sleigh today."

When the kids had all left, the principal remarked, "This is one of the very few days these poor children can actually enjoy Christmas!"

Another time when Santa asked a little girl, "what do you want for Christmas this year?" She sadly replied, "Could you please bring my mom home for Christmas?"

Other Events

We have also been doing the Tree Lighting Ceremony at Benham Grove the Sunday before Thanksgiving each year. Hours and hours of performing in the Santa Cabin at Washington Township's Woodland Heights Christmas Walks, etc.

Needless to say the true spirit of Christmas is in giving—how well we have learned this precious lesson over 47 years as *The Clauses.*

THREE CHRISTMAS HAIKUS
BY VIRGINIA EVERS

Luminaries

Snowflakes falling down
Candles flickering nearby
Lights guide the Christ Child.

Gifts

Bright shining boxes
Which one is your favorite?
A warm loving hug!

Santa

Sleigh bells ringing loud
Reindeer prancing on the roof
Children are awake!

FOR THE CHILDREN
BY DON PEACOCK

As he sat in the third to last pew listening to the pastor give the opening prayer for the Christmas Eve services, he was torn between the services and his feelings about having lost his wife a few months before. She had been his support and his purpose for the thirty-five years they had been married. He was still trying to figure out how to reorient his life amidst the loneliness he felt, but the loneliness was extremely overpowering at times. Getting back to church was the first big step for him in this direction. She had always been the one who insisted on church every week, even when he suggested they do something else once in a while on Sunday morning.

He found it felt good to hear the hymns and the prayers again. He had really missed church for the three months his wife suffered and finally passed away. After the services ended and he was leaving the church, the pastor, standing at the door to say goodbye to the members of the congregation, took his hand and said they were all grieving and praying with him over the loss of his wife.

The pastor asked how he was doing and if the church could do anything for him at this time. This was an instantaneous reminder of the services the church had provided at his wife's funeral as the memories flooded back and he tried to regain his self control. The pastor commented, "Jim, I would like you to meet Mr. Benden, one of our newer members. He is Director of the orphanage over on Third Street. Mr. Benden, this is Jim Jacobsen, one of our long time members." Jim looked over a little uncertain at the man standing there and then reached over to shake his hand.

Mr. Benden, "Please call me Herbert", made some consoling remarks about Jim's loss and then said that if they would pardon him he needed to get over to the orphanage. Jim asked him where on Third Street it was located. It turned out that Jim's apartment was in the same direction, so the two wound up walking together for the first four blocks.

As they walked along Mr. Benden asked if Jim needed anything, further stating that he would be glad to do anything he could that would help.

Jim responded that he was doing as well as he could for the time being. "I'm slowly starting to get back into some things I used to do, even though they seem to mean a lot less now."

"Well, keep my offer in mind, please."

Without thinking Jim asked, "Is there anything I can do for you, sir?"

"We have a Christmas party for the orphans tomorrow. If you feel like it you could come over and help us with it. We start at noon with a special meal and then give out what presents we have. It's one of the most important days of the year for the kids and we like to do it up as best we can afford. None of these kids have anything in the way of family. Only what they have here in the orphanage. We have five pairs of siblings. If you would like to help us tomorrow we would greatly appreciate it."

"Thanks. I will think about it tonight," responded Jim as he broke away and headed into his apartment building.

Once he was inside and settled on his living room sofa the feelings of loss for his wife started to overwhelm him again. He knew it would take a long time for this to end, if it ever did. After several minutes of quietly crying, Jim knew that he had to do something to break his thoughts. Then he realized what he needed to do. He walked across the room, picked up his cell phone and dialed information. When he got the number he wanted he immediately dialed it. After three rings it was answered and a woman's voice said, "Third Street Orphanage. How may I help you?"

"I would like to talk to Mr. Benden please."

"He's busy right now. Can I have him call you back in about ten minutes?"

"Certainly," said Jim and then proceeded to give her his cell number. He then asked about how many orphans were in their facility.

She replied, "We have twenty-five right now, aged from four to twelve. They are mostly under the age of ten. There are ten girls and fifteen boys. Oh, here comes Mr. Bender now. I will put him on the phone for you."

"Thank you," Jim said quickly.

"This is Herbert Benden. What can I do for you?"

"This is Jim Jacobsen. We met at the church this morning. You asked me if I would like to help you tomorrow. The answer is yes. Whatever I can do."

"That is just great of you. We really need all the help we can get. We're having the special lunch at noon and opening what Christmas presents we could put together for the kids. We do have at least one present for each one. It would have been great to have more but our funds were very limited this year. We can only do so much."

Jim quickly responded, "Maybe I can do something about that before I come over. I'll see you about ten in the morning."

"Anything you can do will be greatly appreciated. We really need the help. See you tomorrow."

Jim went out to his mini-van and headed for the local Toys-R-Us. When he got there he took a cart and started through the store, carefully picking selected items off the shelves. When the cart was full Jim took it over to the checkout area, parked it, and told them he was going back for more. He got a second cart and took off down the other side of the store.

After he had four carts full, approximately fifty items of all sizes, he got some help and rolled the four carts up to the checkout as people scattered to the other three checkout lines. Four hundred and seventy five dollars later he had finished with checkout and started leading a caravan of four carts to his vehicle. Once he got all of it in his mini-van he thanked the three guys who helped roll them out, gave them each a nice tip and headed down the street to a gift wrapping store he had seen earlier.

The eyes of the people working at the wrapping store got great big when fifty packages started coming in the door. Then they got started and very quickly had the gifts wrapped with age-group gifts being color coded by the paper and bow used. When they were all done, fifty gifts were again loaded into the mini-van and Jim headed home for the night, but then he detoured to the bakery and bought an assortment of ten pies for dessert the next day. Finally, he headed for home and bed for the night, feeling somewhat more chipper than he had for some time, knowing he was doing something very worthwhile.

The next morning Jim woke up feeling more refreshed and excited than he had in many a month. He hurriedly showered and dressed, fixed some cereal and coffee for breakfast before he started on what he had to do for the day. The first thing was to reload the pies in his minivan. The toys had been left there overnight so everything was almost ready to go. Jim knew he was expected about ten o'clock but he wanted to get to the orphanage a little earlier so he could get everything unloaded and ready for the party. This was particularly true since Mr. Bender did not yet know what he was bringing.

A little after 9:00 Jim hopped into his loaded vehicle and headed over to the orphanage. Ten minutes later he pulled into the small parking lot and found a space for his minivan. He then headed into the building to find Mr. Benden's office.

Once there the two sat down to talk about what was to be done. Mr. Benden started to go over a number of side jobs that he thought Jim could help with but as the discussion progressed and he found out what Jim had brought, the discussion veered to totally different things. At the mention of the gifts that Jim had brought Mr. Bender put forth a totally unexpected prospect.

"Jim, how would you like to be Santa Claus this afternoon? You know the color coding on the presents you brought so that the kids will get the appropriate-age presents plus the kids don't know you so they won't recognize 'Santa's' voice like they did last year. How about it?"

"I wasn't quite prepared for that job. Do you think your Santa suit will fit me? You do realize I have never done anything like that before? That's an intimidating request. Yes, I'll do it with one proviso, that you be the chief elf that gives me the names as the kids come up to talk to me. Do we have a deal?"

"Absolutely. Absolutely. I will be the tallest elf you have ever seen and the kids will get a kick out of it. Let's go get you ready for your gig. I can see right off that we will need at least three pillows to fatten you up enough."

With that they headed for one of the back storerooms in order for both of them to get ready. They found that the Santa suit worked perfectly for Jim and that they only needed two pillows. Jim kept muttering about how he must have put on some weight. The elf setup for Mr. Benden was another matter. An elf outfit for a six foot man is hard to accomplish, so they settled for a colorful vest and a spare Santa hat. It worked fairly well and they knew the kids would talk about it for the whole next year.

Finally at a quarter to twelve everything was ready. The uniforms were on, the presents were around the tree, the food was cooked, and Herb Benden was building Jim up so he wouldn't get cold feet. As the two of them entered the dining room with all twenty-five kids seated around the tables, a great burst of applause was raised, followed closely by peals of laughter at the sight of Benden.

The word, preceded by a prayer, was given and the food started flowing into the room. Individual plates filled with good food: Christmas turkey, stuffing, mashed potatoes and gravy, and a big salad of Romaine lettuce. There was much cheering and pounding of tables while this was accomplished and then the hall got surprisingly quiet as the eating started. Jim and Herb sat quietly, nodding to each other as the kids ate, knowing that the best part was yet to come.

Everyone could feel the excitement increasing as the food disappeared from the plates and the expectation of what Santa had brought took over. Finally, the time arrived. Santa led the parade into the next room where the Christmas tree and the presents had been placed. None of the kids had been allowed in this room before eating, so the surprise was complete. The kids were obviously awed by the number of presents surrounding the tree. In fact, the five foot tree almost disappeared in the midst of them.

Then, all at once, the kids all stood up at the same time, almost as if on order, and started applauding and cheering. 'Santa' walked over to his chair, sat down, and looked up at his extra tall elf and said, "Let's get started before they all explode and particularly before I do."

The "elf" beckoned to a little boy who proceeded to approach, tentatively at first, then fairly leaping onto Santa's lap. The elf just barely had time to whisper, "Ron, five and a half years old."

Santa Jim asked the little guy, "Have you been a good boy, Ron?"

"Yes, Santa" came the quick reply.

"Then I have a present for you. I picked it out just for you."

Ron started to bounce, took the present hastily, as if someone would take it away from him. He then got down and ran back to his chair. Santa had to call him back in order to give him two more presents, and then allowed him to go back and start opening all of them.

This procedure went on through twenty kids. At this point a shy little girl approached Santa and was lifted up onto his lap. At the question of being good or not she looked down and softly said, "I've tried to be, Santa."

He asked the little girl how long she had been in the orphanage. She replied four years, ever since she was two years old. At this point a tear of joy rolled down Santa's cheek and he proceeded to give the little girl her three presents. The tear of joy was because he knew he was doing something so nice for kids who really had nothing. He could tell by the children's reactions how important all of this was to them.

Jim finished up by giving out the presents to the four kids who were over the age of ten. The four showed their appreciation in different ways but it was obvious how much they enjoyed it, while they pretended they still believed in Santa Claus.

In Jim's mind the only thing missing was that his wife could not be there to see him doing all of this. Then as he watched all of the kids with their presents he decided that maybe she really was there watching from Heaven. At that thought another tear rolled down his cheek as he looked up and said, "Hi, honey. I miss you. I sure wish you could have been here for all of this."